Tower Of Souls

AMY LAURENS

OTHER WORKS

Find other works by the author at www.amylaurens.com

Tower Of Souls

INKLET #50

AMY LAURENS

Inkprint PRESS

www.inkprintpress.com

Print ISBN: 978-1-925825-63-3
eBook ISBN: 9781393381051

www.inkprintpress.com

National Library of Australia Cataloguing-in-Publication Data
Laurens, Amy 1985 –
Tower Of Souls
36 p.
ISBN: 978-1-925825-63-3
Inkprint Press, Canberra, Australia
1. Fiction—Fantasy—General 2. Fiction—Ghost 3. Fiction—Short Stories

First Print Edition: January 2021
Cover photo © Dlee via Pixabay
Cover design © Inkprint Press
Interior art © Amy Laurens

TOWER OF SOULS

ADRENALIN FRISSONED FROM STOMACH to fingertips as I landed on a cold, cobbled floor, the foot-thick door slamming shut behind me, blocking out the festival sounds as suddenly as if I'd died. I hadn't, though; my panting gasps echoed in the absolute darkness of the Tower—until I stopped to wet dry lips and realised someone else was breathing too.

My heart leapt. I scrabbled backward against the door; the long, rattling breaths drew closer.

Something touched my foot. I screamed, flinging myself at the spelled wood that separated me from life. Long splinters tore off in my fingertips and blood soaked my nail beds—and something touched my shoulder.

I froze. I screwed my eyes closed, little panicked breaths my only movement.

"Greetings, Wreath-Bearer."

The whispered voice scraped over me like bones rattling in the wind, and I huddled my face against the door. "Please," I whispered, chest heaving. "Don't hurt me."

Cold fingers trailed down my spine. "We will not hurt you, so long as you bear the wreath."

My fingers convulsed against the splintered door. The wreath. I'd dropped the wreath. I whirled around, slamming my back against the wood. Where had I dropped it? It could be anywhere in the dark, it could be—

Against all odds, the wreath lay at my feet, and I could see it: orange flowers bound into a circle with bright orange ribbons, glowing faintly in the midnight dark. I glanced to where I'd last heard the voice, then snatched the wreath from the ground and hugged it to my chest. "I've got it," I said, voice barely tremouring. "You can't hurt me now. You said."

Voice susurrused around me, buffeting me from all sides. "Cannot hurt you... Will not harm... The wreath... The wreath! ... Lead us on..."

I clutched the wreath tighter. "Who... Who are you?"

The whispers rose again, but before I could make out words the first voice spoke. "You know who we are, and what we require. We are the dead. You will lead, and we will follow."

Licking my lips again, I nodded. "Yes. Lead you." My shoulder blades dug against the door and my chest still heaved. I scrunched my eyes closed against the eternal darkness. Lead the dead. Why me? Why *now*? A sob strangled me as I thought of the sky blue dress tucked away in a closet at my mother's house, a dress I'd never need wear now. One day. Just one more day, and I'd have been safely married.

I swiped furiously at the tears that breached my eyelids. "Yes," I said, more strongly this time. "Yes, I am here to lead you."

I was here to lead them, and lead them I would, because I was part of the Tower now, and no one ever came out of the Tower. If I couldn't lead them to the top, I'd die and become one of them, a restless spirit doomed forever to haunt the Tower until someone came who *could* lead us.

"What... What happens if I lose the wreath?" I asked, eyes still closed.

Soft breezes swept my cheek, my forehead, my hair.

"Freya," the voices whispered my name. "Freya."

My heart hammered in my chest. *"What will happen to me?"*

The first voice, the loudest, replied. "If the wreath is lost, we will make you one of us. Then you will hope that the next Wreath-Bearer succeeds where you will have failed."

I swallowed. It had been nineteen years since the last successful Wreath-Bearer. Chances were not great that I would succeed where many stronger had failed.

I clenched my jaw and hugged the wreath to me, burying my face in the uppermost flowers. They smelled like sap and pollen and death. "How will I know the way?" I murmured, mostly to myself.

But this time, the breath against my cheek was almost warm. "Freya." I could hear the smile in the speaker's voice, but I still clutched the wreath over my heart like a shield. "Open your eyes."

The air hitched in my throat, suddenly too dry to pass with ease. Open my eyes?

Visions of dry, desiccated corpses filled my mind's eye, corpses that shambled and hobbled while strips of decaying flesh hung from their bones —and suddenly opening my eyes was less horrifying than keeping them closed a moment longer.

I looked, and gasped.

Silvered figures danced and swirled in front of me, long hair flying, mouths open wide in silent, delightful laughter. The moment they realised I could see them, they turned, crowding in on me, hands outstretched in welcome.

"Come," they whispered. "Come dance with us. Lead us in the dance."

They whirled off and away, smiling, laughing, eyes bright and shining, and as they divided I saw between them a path, gilded and silver, insubstantial as moonlight, real and solid as hope.

My heart still hammered, but what other choice did I have? With my shoulders, I pushed away from the door that had been gouged by fearful hands innumerable, and stepped onto the shining path.

The wreath exploded into light in my hands, warm and amber like a phoenix. It swirled around me, then moved forward. I followed, and the ghosts of decades past came too.

THE MAKING OF
TOWER OF SOULS

Ah, the Tower! I had such plans for this tower. And maybe one day I'll get around to writing a longer story about what goes on here, or finishing some of the other short stories related to it. This little story doesn't show much of the context, after all.

It's a scary proposition, really: the idea is that in this town, once a year one or more people are randomly snatched off the street and thrown into the Tower in order to lead the souls of the dead (who congregate in the Tower, not by choice) to their eternal rest.

In at least a few of the other false starts, it's made clear that unfortunately, no one has been successful in leading the souls to the very top of the

Tower in quite a long time. The souls are growing restless, and the townspeople desperate for someone, anyone who might succeed.

Let us hope that this time, the quest will end in success, both for our protagonist and the souls in the Tower.

Read more by Amy Laurens!

A FOX OF STORMS AND STARLIGHT

CHAPTER ONE

SIX YEARS AGO, I SAVED a fox in the bush. It was only because my dog died. At the time, it felt like a pretty crappy bargain.

It was the first day of autumn—not by the calendar, but by the fresh bite in the morning air, the golden quality of the light as it lit the main road through town in the mid-afternoon.

Sailor was a big, black shaggy thing, something like a Newfoundland, a lively shadow in the golden light, and I was eleven.

I'm sorry to be starting any story this way, but the fact of the matter is, this where it all began.

I'll spare you the awful details. Enough to say that Sailor had got out of the yard somehow, and had been hit by a smallish truck careening down the highway that split our tiny town in two as it blatantly ignored the speed limit.

I saw it happen.

And although I cradled him in my lap as the smell of burnt-out brakes and hot asphalt and turning leaves filled my nose, his giant, furry black head all of him I could hold, there was nothing I could do.

There was nothing anyone could do.

I knew that, but it didn't stop the knot of frustration and guilt in my chest, or the taste of bile in the back of my throat every time I closed my eyes and saw the truck hitting him, again and again and again.

It took years for that vision to fade.

But that evening, only a few hours after it had happened, everything still felt fresh, and raw.

Sunny, my sister, was only nine at the time. She cried for hours, just sobbing like she'd never breathe right again.

I'd cried a little, at the scene with Sailor's head lying in my lap as his big, brown eye stared up at nothing.

It had been mercifully fast, there was that.

And the driver had copped a massive fine—speeding, reckless driving, I think they even defected his truck—and came to visit us later, a big, pot-bellied man standing on our front verandah, shuffling his royal blue cap round and round and round in his hands as he apologised.

But that evening, with Sunny sobbing her heart out on the couch in the living room and Mum and Dad trying desperately to console her as dinner burned on the stove, I couldn't cry, even though the acrid scent of burning soy sauce, scorching brown sugar and smoking rice wine from the marinade prickled the back of my throat and the corners of my eyes.

I was the eldest, and I had to be responsible.

Possibly, if I'd been just a little more responsible, Sailor wouldn't have died.

So I slipped out the glass slider from the family room to the deck while Sunny cried, glancing up at the two storeys of our moody grey house behind me before jumping down the three steps from the rail-less deck to the lawn, and set out for the gate in the back fence.

I couldn't cry, and I didn't want to add anything to an already chaotic and stressful situation inside—but I couldn't stay there, either.

In the gaps between the gum trees to the west, the sky tinged to red and gold at the horizon, the sun sinking slowly into oblivion. I'm pretty sure I didn't know the word oblivion back then, but I knew what it meant, how it felt—and I craved it, desperately.

Anything would be better than the gaping hole in my chest.

And so, because I didn't know where to find it or how to get there, I stalked through the bush, pushing myself until I breathed hard and my lungs ached and sweat ringed me, chasing the way that hard exercise elevated me over my constantly looping thoughts.

Directly above, dark, heavy clouds obscured the sky, and the air was thick, heavy, humid.

Beneath the smell of dry gum leaves and even drier dirt, I could catch a hint of ozone, and occasionally the wind turned cool for a breath as it gusted against my skin, promising a late evening storm.

I strode harder, faster, outpacing the video looping in my mind of the truck's impact.

When the first drops of rain spat at me from out of the sky, I barely noticed. My skin was filmed with sweat, slick and salty, and the peppering of rainwater bare-ly added to it.

That was at first.

But within minutes, it became clear that those first pattering spits had been the early foreshadowing of a storm darker and more intense than any I remembered.

Thunder rolled across the sky, distant and grumbling at first, a lazy background chorus to the rhythmic melody of the rain as it splattered down on grey-green leaves and red-tinged twigs, turning the silvered bark of an old, dead gum to deep grey and making the spiky, tussocky grass seem oddly luminescent in the dying light.

I stood under a grey gum with stains down its trunk that the rain was turning orange, arms wrapped around myself, shivering hard—and for the briefest instant, thought about not going home.

Mum and Dad would pitch a fit.

And I had to be responsible.

I turned, dark t-shirt plastered to my skin, dark hair sticking to my face and clinging to my neck, and began trudging my way back.

The storm closed over properly, clouds rolling over the horizon and cutting off the thin scythe of blood-coloured sunset, making the bush dark and unwelcoming in the premature night.

Lightning flashed.

Thunder cracked hot on its heels.

I jumped—and stared hard at the gap between two ghost-barked trees, where for a second, I was sure I'd seen a pair of eyes.

Nothing moved.

Nothing except the drenching rain, anyway, weighing down the branches that tossed fitfully in the wind.

My pulse slowly calmed.

The rumours we'd all grown up with, indoctrinated since both, spoke of something strange and dark… but in the forest north of here, in the pines, the plantation—not here, not in the natural, native bush.

I shivered.

The smell of wet dirt and soaked bark rose around me, undercut by eucalypt and ozone.

If anything had the power to wash away the hurt inside me, this storm was it. I tipped my face to the sky, imagining that the rain washing over me had the ability to wash me inside as well, and the raindrops splattered hard on my cheekbones, my chin, my tightly closed eyelids.

More lightning. More thunder, cracking over the constant hiss of the falling rain.

And in the distance, something eerie, lifting the hairs on the back of my neck: a strange kind of high-pitched howl, a cry that rang with moonlight and distance, cutting straight through the noise of the storm.

Bolts of lightning streaked across the sky—one—two—three—in the space of half a second, followed immediately by a growling crack of thunder so immense it vibrated in my chest.

I ducked down instinctively into a crouch.

There, in the corner of my eye...

I froze, crouched with my arms over my head.

The strange cries came again—and they were closer.

I stared hard at the place, low to the ground, where I was sure I'd seen something small, maybe the size of a cat.

Flash. Growl.

Rain spitting down.

There. Right there. A small animal, pointy ears, light coloured chin and throat...

The strange, eerie cries came a third time, and my heart pounded fiercely. Whatever was making the noise, it was close. Really close.

The little creature across from me reacted too, flattening itself to the ground.

My jaw twitched.

My heart pounded.

My fingertips bit into my upper arms.

Stay? Go?

Run? Freeze?

The hairs on my neck prickled again and goosebumps broke out all over me.

Cold dread formed a knot in my stomach.

Something was coming.

Something worse than the storm.

I had to get home.

I made it halfway to standing—and a series of strange, awful noises made me freeze again. They were sharp, clacking, squealing sounds, like someone knocking two echoing stones against each other, interspersed with high-pitched yowling…

The creature in the darkness screamed.

I threw my back against the gumtree behind me, pressing hard against it.

My heart hammered.

I peered back and forth in the dark, eyes wide.

Rain drenched down, but my throat was dry.

My pulse pounded faster.

The little creature screamed again—and as lightning flashed, I saw it on its back, legs slashing wildly as something attacked.

The awful, clicking-yowling noises sounded right in front of me.

I slapped my hands over my ears, gasping. Water ran down my face, getting into my mouth, my eyes.

It was hurting.

Whatever the small thing was, it was getting hurt, and I'd seen enough animals hurting today.

Something in my chest snapped.

I flung myself across the ground, leaping a couple of tussocks and a fallen branch before I crashed to my knees.

I crawled closer, desperate, gasping for air through the heavy curtains of rain.

I couldn't see it. Where?

Somewhere here, near the base of that tree...

The yowling screeched right next to my ear. I cowered against the ground, spiky grass pricking my face, wet-earth smell smothering me—but now, there was a strange mustiness too, a cousin to wet-dog smell.

At the next flash of lightning, I saw it.

The creature was a fox—and something barely visible was attacking it, only the gleam of eye or flicker of teeth visible in the gloom.

But the damage was real enough.

The little fox's side had been opened right up, and in the bright, stark flashes of heavenly electricity, the blood was dark, thinned by the constant rain.

No. No more animals were going to die today.

Not when this time, I could do some-thing about it.

I snatched at a branch on the ground that turned out to be more of a glorified twig, and launched myself toward the creature.

I had no idea what was attacking it, but I screamed and waved my handful of twiggy leaves anyway, batting them in the air over the fox like I knew what I was doing.

The horrible clacking cries ceased abruptly.

With one long, low rumble, the rain began to ebb.

I poised, waiting.

But nothing came.

The attackers were gone.

Still gasping for air, pulse galloping in my throat, I sat next to the fox and shifted it carefully into my lap, realising as I tasted salt that I was crying.

I huddled over, trying to shelter the poor creature from the slackening rain, running my fingers over its wiry cheek—over and over and over and over.

"Please," I sobbed, throat tight and aching, chest constricted. "Please. Please don't die. Please."

Please, I prayed to anything that might be listening. *No more death. Not today.*

Not today.

Another gust of cool air washed over the clearing, taking the last of the rain with it—and lifting the goose-bumps on my arms again.

And as it did, I could have sworn I heard a voice. *Neither do I wish him to die now.*

I shivered, drawing the fox close, like it was a stuffed animal I could hug for comfort—its comfort or mine, I couldn't say. I glanced around the dripping bush, eyes wide. The rumours spoke of an evil presence, and I could easily believe that might be what had attacked the fox.

But a voice? No one had ever mentioned a voice.

There was nothing to be seen, and anyway the voice had sounded kindly—and didn't want the fox to die.

Assuming I hadn't just imagined it, of course. Which, half-drowned by grief, the other half drowned by the storm... An over-active imagination seemed highly likely.

Can you fix him? I thought it hard, though, just in case someone really was listening.

Something shifted in my lap.

Around us, the world stilled, dazed from the storm, but also something more, something watching, something waiting, as the bush held its collective breath.

The only sound was the occasional drip of rainwater from the gum leaves onto a fallen log—no insects, no wind, no rustling of leaves.

Just… stillness.

And the fox, who shivered in my lap.

The clouds tore open, revealing a ragged triangle of stars that glittered in the fox's eye as it blinked open and stared up at me.

My chest snagged.

My throat ached from crying, and a headache was forming in the back of my head.

But the fox blinked up at me—alive.

I ran a finger down it again, from nose to cheek to ear to shoulder, all the way down its side to its thick, bushy tail—and the wound in its side began to close.

Laboriously, it hauled itself to its front legs.

I tried to stop it—"No, it's okay, you can stay here, I'll look after you"—but it lifted its top lip to show half-hearted teeth, and staggered away.

As it did, I thought perhaps its fur began to shrink.

And suddenly, it looked larger in the night—as large as a dog, as large as Sailor…

But I blinked, and it was just a trick of the light, because the creature that darted away into the bushes like nothing was wrong at all was clearly a fox, the size of a large cat or maybe a small beagle, and nothing more.

And if something screamed in the night not long afterward, and the cry sounded horribly, horribly human?

Well.

I was halfway back toward home again by then, and I pressed my fingertips to my lower eyelids and prayed my parents wouldn't murder me for getting home so late.

Keep reading! Head to
www.inkprintpress.com/amylaurens/
stormfoxes/fox/
to buy your copy now!

ABOUT THE AUTHOR

Amy Laurens is an Australian author of fantasy fiction for all ages. She has never been abandoned in a tower of ghostly souls, but her children certainly sound like it sometimes.

Amy has also written the award-winning portal-fantasy *Sanctuary* series about Edge, a 13-year-old girl forced to move to a small country town because of witness protection (the first book is *Where Shadows Rise*), the humorous fantasy *Kaditeos* series, following newly graduated Evil Overlord Mercury as she attempts to acquire a castle, the young adult series *Storm Foxes*, about love and magic and family in small town Australia, and a whole host of non-fiction.

INKLETS

Collect them all! Released on the 1st and 15th of each month.

INKLET #055
Allure
AMY LAURENS

INKLET #056
The LIES We KNOW
LIANA BROOKS

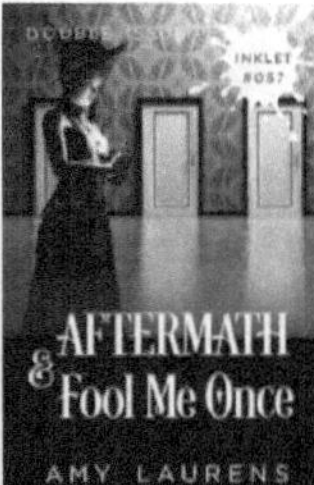

INKLET #057
DOUBLE
AFTERMATH & Fool Me Once
AMY LAURENS

INKLET #058
Purity
An Age Of Unicorns Story
AMY LAURENS

INKLET #059
Saved
AMY LAURENS

INKLET #060
A Kiss is the Secret
AMY LAURENS

INKLET #061
A Changing Tides Story
Fire Bright
AMY LAURENS

INKLET #062
Hades AND Persephone
LIANA BROOKS

INKLET #063
Just So Long As You're Happy
AMY LAURENS

INKLET #064
Theft Of A Lifetime
LIANA BROOKS

INKLET #065
Shoe
AMY LAURENS

INKLET #066
Published AUTHOR
LIANA BROOKS

DOUBLE ISSUE
INKLET #067
THE REMARKABLE INSIGHT OF JELLYBEANS & Understanding
AMY LAURENS

INKLET #068
Desperate Measures
AMY LAURENS

INKLET #069
Rock-a-bye
LIANA BROOKS

INKLET #070
the Other Carly
AMY LAURENS

INKLET #071
By Bioluminescent Light
AMY LAURENS

INKLET #072
Even Villains Grant Wishes
A Heroes & Villains Story
LIANA BROOKS

www.ingramcontent.com/pod-product-compliance
Lightning Source LLC
Chambersburg PA
CBHW032054180726
48284CB00004B/1329